W9-BRN-735

Library of Congress catalog card number: 90-55288
Originally published in French by Les Livres du Dragon d'Or
under the title *La folle journée de Lapin élastique*
Published simultaneously in Canada by HarperCollins, Toronto
First American edition, 1990

The Busy Day of Jack Rabbit

Anne-Marie Dalmais / Pictures by Graham Percy

Farrar Straus Giroux
New York

A persistent ringing wakes Jack Rabbit with a start. He looks at the clock and jumps out of bed. He doesn't have a minute to lose.

Jack gulps down a cup of coffee and puts on a uniform with brass buttons. He grabs a small bag, heaves a mysterious bundle on his shoulder, and hops down the staircase four steps at a time.

Jack dashes into a taxi.

"To the airport!" he orders. "And hurry, my plane is leaving soon." Jack Rabbit is a flight attendant with Open Air Airlines, and a long day of work awaits him.

First he welcomes the passengers on board the airplane with a big smile and helps them get settled.

"Mrs. Hippo, I beg your pardon, allow me to put your bags away," he says.

Once the passengers are seated, the rabbit must be a jack-of-all-trades. He becomes a gym teacher when he demonstrates the safety procedures, using lively gestures to show how to use an oxygen mask and how to get into a life jacket just in case there's an emergency.

After the plane takes off, Jack discovers that two turtledoves on their honeymoon have been seated in separate rows. Jack plays the diplomat and tactfully asks Mr. Heron to change places so the turtledoves may sit together.

Another flight attendant, Katy Cat, has been trying, unsuccessfully, to set up a crib for the baby porcupine. Jack, who is a handyman too, quickly adjusts the rebellious nuts and bolts.

The agile rabbit only needs to slip on an apron to turn into a waiter. He skillfully hands out menus, fruit juice, and soda.

Serving lunch is a tricky task. Jack must keep smiling, even when Mr. Squirrel demands a third dessert and the magpie spills cherry juice all over her neighbor.

The flight across the Atlantic is a long one. To entertain the passengers, Open Air Airlines offers an in-flight movie. Who operates the film projector? Jack, of course!

He distributes the headphones and explains how they work, while Katy pulls the curtains in front of the screen. Then Jack starts the projector and the film begins.

Even while the movie is on, Jack can't relax. Like a school principal, he must repeatedly reprimand the wild boar, who jumps up every two seconds, exclaiming that he cannot get comfortable. Jack finally manages to make him sit down and watch the movie.

Jack steals to the back of the cabin.
"What's in your package?" asks Katy.
"The secret to my relaxation," says Jack.

When the movie is over, the whirlwind of activity starts up at once, and Jack changes jobs again. He becomes a salesman, pushing a cart loaded with watches, chocolates, scarves, and other pretty things down the aisle. It's almost like a department store on wheels.

Suddenly, Jack finds himself nose to nose with the voluminous Mrs. Hippo. Of course, he is very courteous about this mishap, and walks backwards to get out of her way, wearing his most charming smile.

Once out of the traffic jam, Jack closes shop.

But no sooner is he finished than he discovers yet another task awaiting him. The captain has invited the famous engineer Mr. Rooster to visit, and Jack must guide him to the cockpit.

Jack a geography teacher? For some curious passengers, he patiently points out the various sights.

His work as a teacher is not over, though. Jack instructs the passengers how to fill out their customs forms, and he points out that they must turn back their watches six hours.

Finally, the rabbit who since dawn has been hopping and leaping, going and coming, sits down!

But only for five minutes—as long as it takes for the plane to land in New York.

In a jiffy, Jack is standing at the top of the ramp. He looks as fresh as when he greeted the passengers early that morning in Paris.

"Goodbye. I hope you had a nice trip," he says as each passenger leaves the plane.

At last Jack has finished work as a flight attendant. With his luggage and the mysterious package, he hops into a taxi.

Because of the time change, it is only two o'clock in the afternoon. Jack meets his friend Mr. Raccoon to play a round of golf. That is why he brought his favorite clubs, carefully wrapped, all the way from Paris.

Jack and the raccoon play for many hours. So you see, Jack Rabbit's busy day is not really over.